Crinkleroot's
NATURE ALMANAC

For Anna, Alex, and Hatcher

Simon & Schuster Books for Young Readers

An imprint of Simon & Schuster Children's Publishing Division

1230 Avenue of the Americas, New York, New York 10020

Copyright © 1999 by Jim Arnosky

SIMON & SCHUSTER BOOKS FOR YOUNG READERS is a trademark of Simon & Schuster.

Book design by Heather Wood and Jim Arnosky

The text for this book is set in Fairfield Medium.

The illustrations are rendered in watercolor.

Printed in Hong Kong

1   3   5   7   9   10   8   6   4   2

Library of Congress Cataloging-in-Publication Data

Arnosky, Jim.

Crinkleroot's nature almanac / by Jim Arnosky. — 1st ed.

p.   cm.

Summary : Crinkleroot the forest dweller describes the changes
that take place in animals and plants throughout the four seasons.

ISBN 0-689-80534-9

1. Animals—Juvenile literature. 2. Nature study—Activity programs—Juvenile literature.
3. Seasons—Juvenile literature. [1. Seasons. 2. Animals. 3. Nature study.] I. Title.

QL49.A772 1999   508—dc21   98-27191   CIP   AC

Crinkleroot's
NATURE ALMANAC

Jim Arnosky

SIMON & SCHUSTER BOOKS FOR YOUNG READERS

History of Crinkleroot

Nobody really knows how old Crinkleroot is. He says he is much older than ten and a lot younger than one thousand. I myself wasn't much older than ten when I began telling his story, back in the 1970s.

I drew the very first pictures of Crinkleroot, and his friends Sassafrass and Walking Stick, late one evening in Pennsylvania. My family and I were living in a cabin at the foot of a wooded mountain. Don't ask me how I knew what he looked like—I just knew. His eyes and nose and long beard flowed out of my pen onto paper. I knew just what kind of hat he wore and where to put a feather in his hair.

Crinkleroot was named after the wildflower, crinkleroot. It grows in wooded places up on hillsides and down beside streams. I have found the wildflower crinkleroot many times while walking and exploring. When my family and I moved from Pennsylvania to Vermont, crinkleroot was one of the first wildflowers we discovered growing around our new home.

I've been drawing Crinkleroot for many years, following his antics in the woods and fields. This almanac is made up of new drawings and old. Some pictures and stories in it go back to the early days of Crinkleroot and me.

I find Crinkleroot as fascinating as the world of nature he explores in his long walks. I hope you enjoy this new look at an old friend, as he guides you through the seasons in a very special nature almanac.

Table of Contents

Crinkleroot's Song

Music and lyrics by Jim Arnosky

He has a long gray beard and bright red hair,
And he carries a walking stick shaped like a bear.
He's not very tall but he needn't be,
Because a snake on his head makes him six foot three.
That's right!
A snake on his head makes him six foot three.

Chorus:

Crinkleroot, Crinkleroot,
Walking Stick and snake.
Crinkleroot, Crinkleroot,
Three good friends they make.

He can howl like a coyote and sing like a bird,
And he speaks fluent caterpillar, every word.
When he meets a mountain lion, he don't run in fear.
He just roars "Howdy Do!" in the lion's ear.
That's right!
Roars "Howdy Do!" in the lion's ear.

Chorus:

Crinkleroot, Crinkleroot,
Knows what the animals say.
Crinkleroot, Crinkleroot,
Tell us what you heard today.

Deep in the forest 'neath the tallest tree,
Lives as fine an old gentleman that you can meet.
He treats wild creatures like he'd treat you and me,
'Cause he was born in a tree and raised by bees.
That's right!
Born in a tree and raised by bees.

Chorus:

Crinkleroot, Crinkleroot,
Watching the wild things play.
Crinkleroot, Crinkleroot,
Tell us what you saw today.

Spring

Hello! My name is Crinkleroot. I was born in a tree and raised by bees. I can hear a fox turn in the forest and spot a mole hole on a mountain. I can track a flea through the fur on a bear's back. I can whistle in a hundred languages and speak caterpillar, turtle, and salamander too!

Where I live, deep in the forest, the trees grow so tall they touch the sky. And sometimes, when I look up at the treetops, I can feel the world slowly turning.

Day by day, week by week, month by month, I love to watch the seasons change. Summer. Autumn. Winter. Spring.

Right now it's springtime, and everything in the forest is waking up after a long winter rest.

The old bee tree is humming with activity. Hundreds of worker bees are out, buzzing about, searching for the very first spring flowers. Flowers provide the nectar and pollen that bees need to make honey.

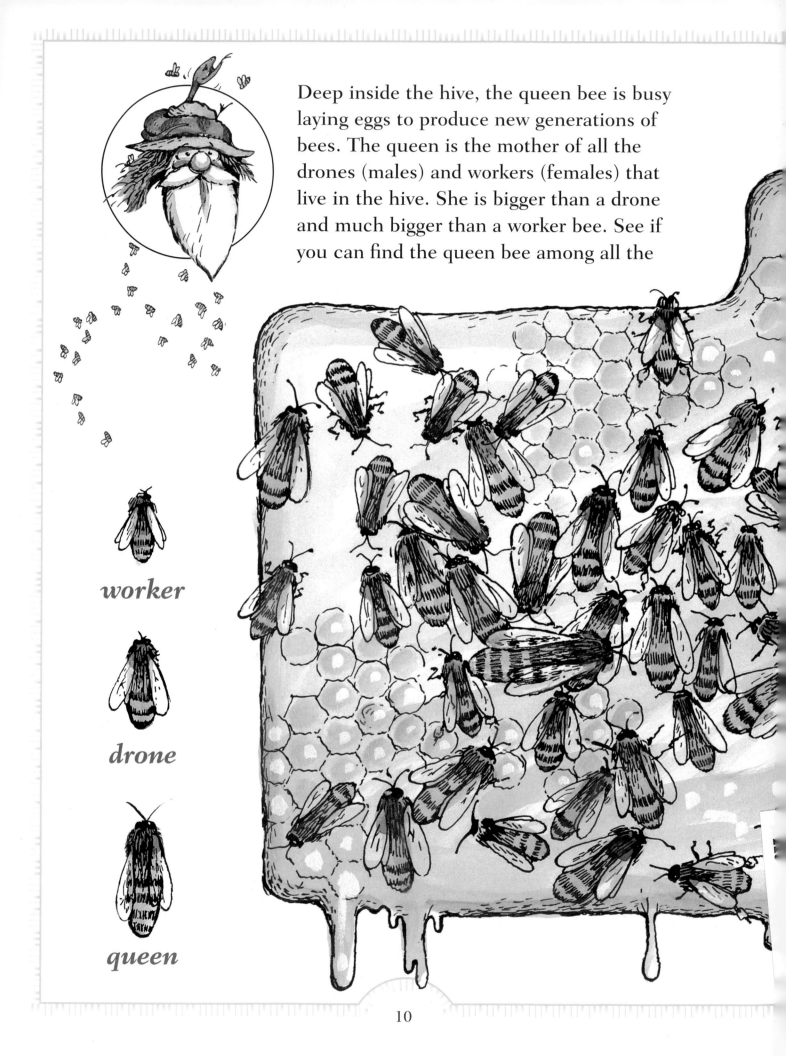

Deep inside the hive, the queen bee is busy laying eggs to produce new generations of bees. The queen is the mother of all the drones (males) and workers (females) that live in the hive. She is bigger than a drone and much bigger than a worker bee. See if you can find the queen bee among all the

worker

drone

queen

bees on this honeycomb. Remember, she is the largest
bee in the hive.

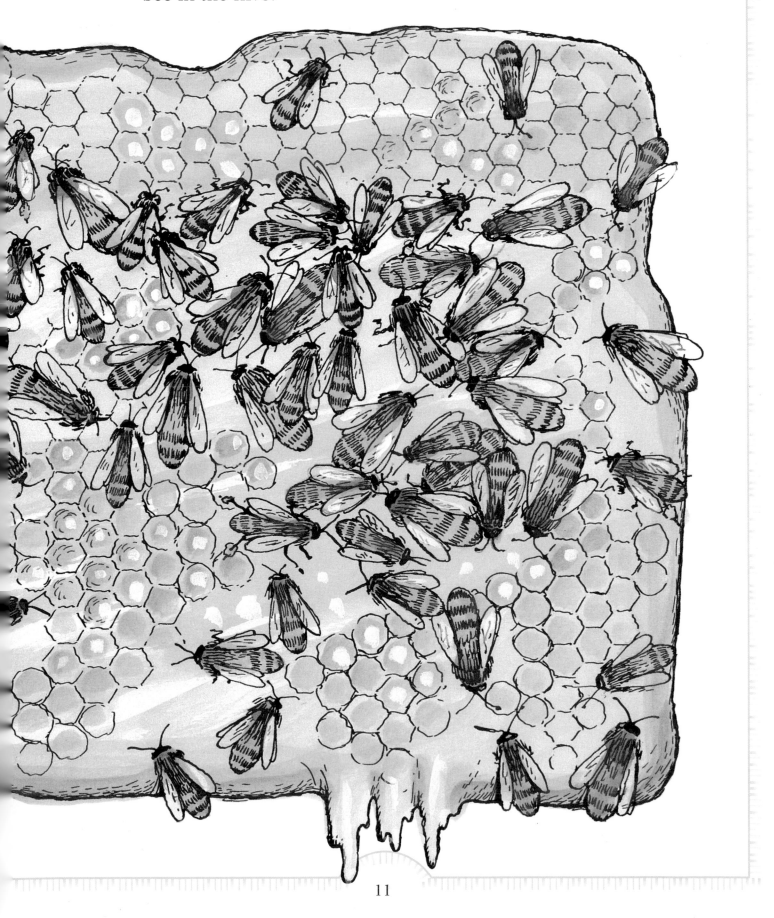

Spring Wildflowers

Look at these wildflowers poking through the leafy soil. You can find wildflowers growing in the little wild places around your home, anywhere that hasn't been mowed. Remember, don't pick wildflowers, just look at them, and they will appear each year in the same places.

All plants and animals grow best in their natural surroundings. Some plants, like this arrowhead, grow right in water.

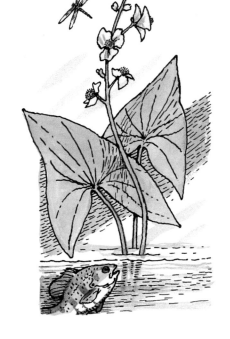

The moccasin orchid grows in bogs, and in rocky woods where the soil is moist. Whoever named this flower thought it looked like a soft, slipperlike shoe.

Wild strawberries grow best in sunny open places.

Trout lilies grow along the shady banks of streams.

I grow best wherever I can stretch out my arms and breathe fresh clean air!

Planting Popcorn

My! All this hunting for wildflowers has given me the munchies. Come inside my cabin while I pop some corn.

Popcorn is my favorite snack. I grow it in my garden. Do you know how popcorn grows? I'll show you.

Of course, the best place for popcorn to grow is outdoors in a cornfield. There, rows and rows of corn plants stretch tall in the sunlight, and wind gently blows the plants' tassel tops, distributing pollinating seeds from one plant to another.

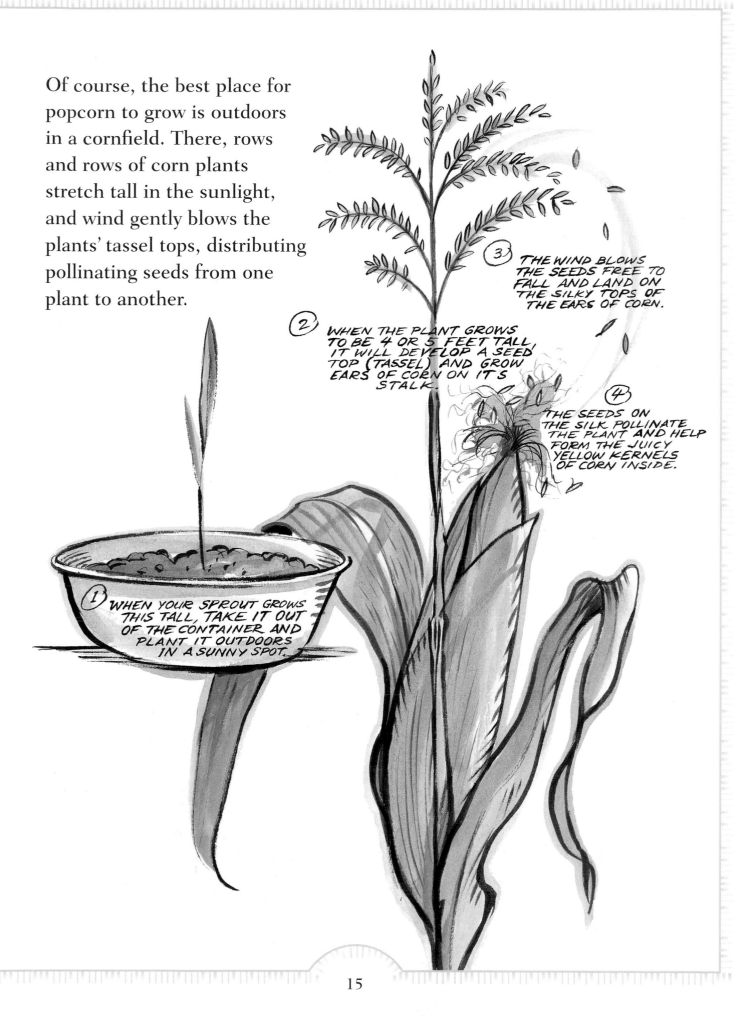

③ THE WIND BLOWS THE SEEDS FREE TO FALL AND LAND ON THE SILKY TOPS OF THE EARS OF CORN.

② WHEN THE PLANT GROWS TO BE 4 OR 5 FEET TALL, IT WILL DEVELOP A SEED TOP (TASSEL) AND GROW EARS OF CORN ON ITS STALK.

④ THE SEEDS ON THE SILK POLLINATE THE PLANT AND HELP FORM THE JUICY YELLOW KERNELS OF CORN INSIDE.

① WHEN YOUR SPROUT GROWS THIS TALL, TAKE IT OUT OF THE CONTAINER AND PLANT IT OUTDOORS IN A SUNNY SPOT.

A Crinkleroot Nature Quiz

We've seen how different wildflowers and plants grow best in their natural surroundings, or habitats. The same is true for animals.

How many wild animals can you think of that are found only in certain habitats?

Here are three to get you started.

Woodpeckers are found in forests and woods where there are plenty of rotted limbs and tree trunks to peck. They peck away loose bark and dead wood, in search of insects to eat.

Loons are found only on large rivers or lakes where there is plenty of room for these big, heavy birds to take off and land, and where there is plenty of fish to catch and eat.

The snowy owl lives in the snowy north where the landscape is low and flat and the owl can spot its prey from far away.

Summer

Summer is a time of misty mornings and sunny afternoons. In the forest around my cabin, turkeys perch in trees, and colorful snakes rest on hot, dry rocks.

This is a secret place I like to come to and rest. Sometimes I fish, and sometimes I just watch quietly. Often a deer will tiptoe down to the stream for a drink. On warm summer evenings, I listen to the splashes of trout leaping after insects.

A kingfisher frequents this part of the stream. It perches on an overhanging branch to watch the water for minnows. Tiny minnows swim in the stream and sparkle in the ripples. See the kingfisher dive for its supper of minnows. How many minnows can you see?

Here's another puzzle for your eyes. I've been watching this toad for a long while now, and I've seen it catch a few bugs. How many bugs can you see it catch?

Toads are really animals of dusk and nighttime. All the animals in the picture with me are nighttime creatures.

They sleep or hide all day, waiting until it's dark to move about.

Answers: (a) great horned owl / (b) screech owl / (c) opossum / (d) flying squirrel / (e) bat / (f) raccoon / (g) skunk / (h) salamander / (i) wood rat

Wildlife Signs
in Spring and Summer

One way to know for sure that animals have been moving about is to look for their signs. When you and I walk in the woods, we leave signs that we've been there—our footprints! Animals also leave marks and tracks that show where they have been and what they have been doing.

The best places to look for wildlife signs are around water. Animals are attracted to streams and ponds, park fountains, and even damp patches of grass. There they find water to drink and food to eat.

This pond was actually created by wildlife. It is a beaver's pond. Can you see the chewed and fallen trees? Beavers have sharp teeth and can gnaw down a tree! Chewed-down trees and gnawed-off twigs are good beaver signs to look for.

BEAVER

CHEWED TREE

FLAT TAIL

🐾 BEAVERS ARE IN THE SAME ANIMAL FAMILY AS MUSKRATS, MICE, AND SQUIRRELS.

🐾 THEY CAN LIVE ANYWHERE THERE IS WATER TO DAM AND A HEAVY GROWTH OF TREES AND BUSHES TO EAT.

🐾 BEAVERS CAN GROW TO BE VERY BIG. SOME WEIGH AS MUCH AS 70 POUNDS.

🐾 A CLOSE RELATIVE OF THE BEAVER, THE MUSKRAT, MAY LIVE IN STREAMS OR MARSHES NEAR YOU!

Beavers create a pond by damming up a stream, using branches, sticks, and mud. A dam like this is a sure sign that beavers are living in the ponds. Beavers are slow and clumsy on land but graceful and swift in water. They build their dams to flood areas so they can swim around rather than walk.

Whenever a beaver fells a tree that is too heavy to drag to the water, it chews the tree into small logs and rolls each one into the pond. The beaver then pushes the floating log to wherever it is needed. Sometimes a beaver gets lucky and the tree falls right into the pond. Beavers use logs and chewed-off branches to build their homes, or lodges.

LODGE ►

◄ ENTRANCE

FLOW

MUDDY BOTTOM

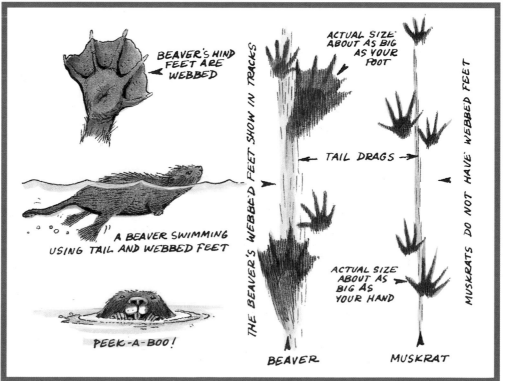

BEAVER'S HIND FEET ARE WEBBED

A BEAVER SWIMMING USING TAIL AND WEBBED FEET

PEEK-A-BOO!

THE BEAVER'S WEBBED FEET SHOW IN TRACKS

ACTUAL SIZE ABOUT AS BIG AS YOUR FOOT

← TAIL DRAGS →

ACTUAL SIZE ABOUT AS BIG AS YOUR HAND

MUSKRATS DO NOT HAVE WEBBED FEET

BEAVER

MUSKRAT

Another beaver sign to look for is the beaver's large webbed footprints.

Here are more webbed footprints, but these aren't beaver tracks.

These tracks were made by an otter.

Otters are more at home in water than on land.

OTTER

WEBBED HIND FEET

🐾 OTTERS ARE IN THE WEASEL FAMILY. SO ARE MINKS, BADGERS, AND SKUNKS. (AND WEASELS!)

🐾 OTTERS CAN GROW TO BE 20 POUNDS OR MORE.

🐾 IF YOU LIVE NEAR A RIVER, YOU MAY HAVE AN OTTER LIVING NEAR YOU!

🐾 IF YOU LIVE NEAR A WOODLOT, LOOK FOR SOME OF OTTER'S WEASEL RELATIVES.

WHEEEE!

Much of an otter's life is spent in the quiet, murky, underwater world. An otter can outswim a big bass or trout! Can you see the otter catching the fish in the picture below?

Otters are carefree critters. They play for hours, sliding down muddy spots on the pond bank and splashing into the water. You may have seen otters sliding at the zoo. Otters swim and play all day long, then sleep soundly through the night to restore their energy for another very active day.

It's such a nice night to stroll in the moonlight. Listen! I can hear an otter sleeping somewhere, snoring away. If you are very quiet, you can hear some of the many sounds of a warm summer —insects chirping, an owl hooting, a fox barking. If you stand very still and close your eyes, you may even be able to hear the summer leaves whispering in the soft, summer breeze.

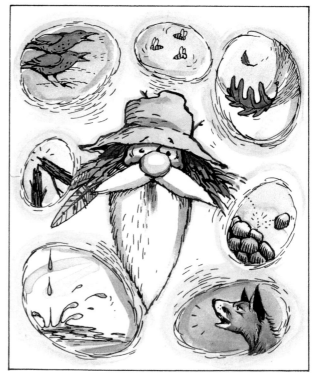

Autumn

Autumn is the time of year when the green leaves turn colors and fall to the ground. Everywhere you look— leaves! Reds and yellows, golds and nutty browns.

Making an Autumn Leaf Book

In autumn, I like to collect different leaves and use them to make a leaf book.

First I trace each leaf's shape on a piece of paper. Then I color the leaf shape the same color as the autumn leaf.

When I have enough colorful drawings to make my leaf book, I tie the papers together with yarn.

You can do the same thing. Then you can show your family and friends all the leaves in your autumn leaf book.

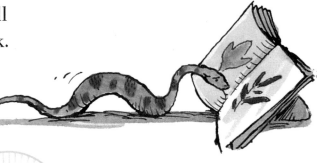

Animals spend autumn eating all
they can to fatten up in preparation
for the coming winter. This opossum is out searching
for food. An opossum will eat anything from earthworms,
frogs, and snails to ripe berries. All of the animals and
plants hidden in this picture are in the opossum's diet.

Building a Bird Feeder

One way you can help wildlife get ready for winter is to build a seed feeder for the birds and squirrels.

Seed feeders are easy to make. My favorite is one I made from empty milk cartons. All the things you need for your feeder can be found around the house. Look for three empty milk cartons, one long stick (about 18 inches long), glue, twine, a pair of safety scissors, and some brown paint. Make sure you ask an adult to help you!

A Crinkleroot Nature Quiz

You never know who may drop by your seed feeder. All of these hungry wild critters eat seeds as part or all of their diets.

Can you name them all?

One bird that's apt to come by your feeder is the crow. Autumn is the time when crows congregate and form large winter flocks. A flock of crows can be a noisy bunch, especially when they spot one of their enemies. Crows will chase foxes, coyotes, hawks, and owls. If you hear a flock of crows and see them all circling a certain tree, you know they have located an owl in daytime. They will call and dive and badger the owl until it goes deep into the woods to hide.

Owls usually come out only at night. But I can locate owls during the daytime, too. How? When an owl eats a mouse, it swallows it whole—tail and all. The owl's stomach digests everything except the mouse bones and fur. The bones and fur form a ball that the owl coughs up and out onto the ground. These balls of bones and fur are called owl pellets. That's how I find owls in the daytime. I keep an eye out for owl pellets.

←OWL PELLET

Owl pellets collect on the ground around trees where owls hide and sleep during the day. If you have trees in your yard, look for owl pellets under them. Don't touch them or pick them up. You can see they are made of mouse fur and bones just by looking at them. If you find some, look up in the tree and see if you can spot an owl sleeping in a branch.

Here is a tree with owl pellets under it. How many pellets can you count? Can you find the owl in the branches?

Wildlife Signs
in Autumn and Winter

A patch of autumn woods is a good place to look for deer. Deer are shy and like to stay hidden much of the day among the trees and shadows of the woodland.

WHITETAIL DEER

FLASHING WARNING →

WHITE PATCH UNDER TAIL

BABY DEER ARE CALLED "FAWNS"

🐾 WHITETAIL DEER ARE NAMED FOR THE WHITE PATCH UNDER THEIR TAILS. WHEN DEER ARE FRIGHTENED THEY FLASH THEIR WHITE TAIL PATCHES TO WARN THE OTHER DEER.

🐾 DEER ARE IN THE SAME ANIMAL FAMILY AS ELK, MOOSE, CARIBOU, AND MULE DEER.

🐾 DEER DO NOT LIKE FORESTS OF TALL TREES. THEY PREFER WOODS OF YOUNG, SMALL TREES AND OPEN FIELDS. THEY EAT TWIGS, ACORNS, AND GRASSES.

In the woods, deer eat twigs, buds, and seeds. In autumn they feast on fallen acorns. Deer tramp trails all through the woods as they move from feeding spot to feeding spot.

This is a deer trail. You can see the deer's pointed hoof tracks pressed in the mush of trampled leaves and soil.

All summer long the male deer, called "bucks," have been growing antlers on their heads. During the time they are growing, the antlers are covered with a layer of velvety skin.

In autumn, when bucks' antlers are fully grown, the velvety covering dries up and begins to peel. The bucks scrape it off by rubbing their antlers against the bark of small trees and bushes. This creates worn, smooth spots on the trees' wood, called "buck rubs." You may have noticed buck rubs in your autumn woods.

Bucks use their sharp, freshly cleaned and polished antlers to fight each other to see who will mate with the female deer, called "does."

After the mating season is over, the antlers fall off. Each buck is left with two small smooth spots on his head, where new antlers will begin to grow again in spring.

Antlers that have fallen off are eaten by mice, squirrels, and other hungry forest nibblers. But until they are eaten, they lie on the forest floor. A buck has shed his antlers in this patch of woods. Can you find them? Sometimes antlers fall off one at a time, so you might not find the set together.

The most commonly seen signs of deer and other animals are their footprints. In autumn, when deer are very active and on the move, you can find their tracks everywhere… in the woods, on the banks of streams, in harvested cornfields, even in your own backyard!

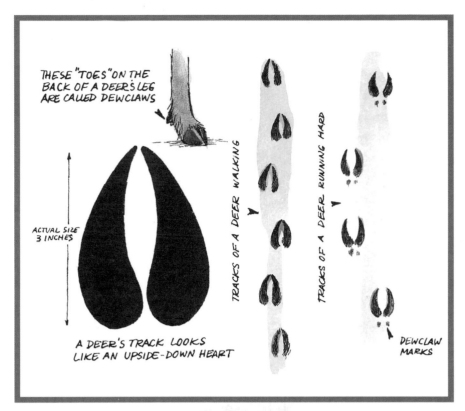

THESE "TOES" ON THE BACK OF A DEER'S LEG ARE CALLED DEWCLAWS

ACTUAL SIZE 3 INCHES

A DEER'S TRACK LOOKS LIKE AN UPSIDE-DOWN HEART

TRACKS OF A DEER WALKING

TRACKS OF A DEER RUNNING HARD

DEWCLAW MARKS

Here are the tracks of another animal that you may find in all the places you find deer. Can you guess what animal made them?

If you said raccoon, you are right! Raccoons eat anything they catch or find. They come to the water to hunt for crayfish, frogs, snails, and freshwater clams. Like many wild animals, raccoons are mostly nocturnal. That means they are more active at night than during the day.

Raccoons are expert climbers. Often you will see their tracks leading right up to a tree that the raccoon has climbed. Sometimes, in the daytime, raccoons climb out onto a sunny tree limb and sleep. I've seen raccoons sleeping this way, with all four legs dangling down.

RACCOON

🐾 A RACCOON CAN BE BROWN OR GRAY WITH A MASK OF BLACK FUR ON ITS FACE AND BLACK RINGS ON ITS TAIL.

🐾 MOST RACCOONS WEIGH BETWEEN 10 POUNDS AND 15 POUNDS.

🐾 RACCOONS GRUNT, GROWL, HISS, AND SOMETIMES THEY CHUCKLE.

🐾 A RACCOON'S TEETH ARE AS BIG AS A DOG'S TEETH — ONLY MUCH SHARPER.

Here are lots of raccoon tracks in the mud. Follow them and see what they tell you. What did the big raccoons catch and eat? How many small raccoons were there?

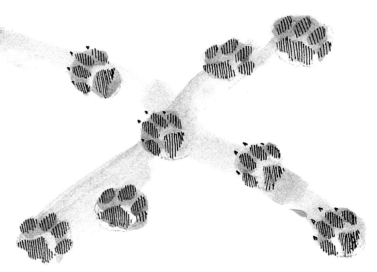

Raccoon tracks are easy to identify. They look like no other animal's tracks. On the other hand, cat tracks and dog tracks are very similar and are often mistaken for one another.

TRACKS OF A WALKING CAT

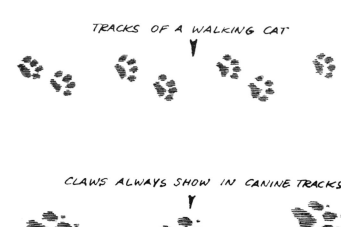

The secret to telling dog tracks from cat tracks is this: Cat tracks rarely show any claw marks; dog tracks always show claw or nail marks.

CLAWS ALWAYS SHOW IN CANINE TRACKS

SEE HOW THE CLAWS SHOW IN THE LUNGE.

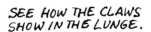

TRACKS OF A CAT JUMPING AFTER A MOUSE

The reason for this is that cats have retractable claws—which means they can fold their claws up and away—and dogs do not.

If you see cat tracks that change from clawless prints to prints with claw marks, you have found a place where a cat has lunged after a mouse and tried to catch it.

The same is true for wild relatives of cats and dogs. For instance, a bobcat is a wildcat that lives in forests, canyons, and desert areas. A bobcat's paw is about two times the size of a house cat's paw. Like a cat, a bobcat's prints are clawless, until it lunges to catch something.

ACTUAL SIZE ABOUT 2 INCHES

The fox and the dog belong to the same animal family, the canine family. A dog's footprints and a fox's footprints look very much alike. Both always show claw marks in their footprints.

ACTUAL SIZE 2½ INCHES

The only difference between a fox trail and a dog trail is this: When a fox walks, it places one foot directly in front of the other, leaving a trail much narrower than a dog's. If you see a trail of doglike tracks that lie in a straight line, you are looking at fox tracks.

BOBCAT

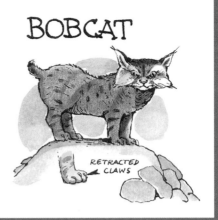

RETRACTED CLAWS

- BOBCATS ARE NAMED FOR THEIR SHORT, BOBBED TAILS.

- BOBCATS CAN GROW TO BE TWICE THE SIZE OF A HOUSE CAT.

- THEY ARE IN THE SAME ANIMAL FAMILY AS LIONS, TIGERS, COUGARS, AND HOUSE CATS.

- BOBCATS WILL EAT SMALL ANIMALS, RABBITS, AND BIRDS.

RED FOX

- THE RED FOX IS A REDDISH ORANGE FOX WITH A WHITE TIPPED TAIL.

- FOXES LIVE IN DENS THEY DIG OUT IN FIELDS OR ON THE EDGES OF WOODS.

- SOMETIMES IN THE WINTER FOXES WILL SLEEP IN THE OPEN AIR IN THE MIDDLE OF AN OPEN FIELD.

- A FOX BARK SOUNDS LIKE THE "YIP" OF A SMALL DOG.

Winter

As the weather gets colder, food in the forest is harder to find. Raccoons make nightly visits to my garbage pile. Deer roam farther into the forest, looking for food and shelter from the wind. Birds congregate around my feeder. I love to fill it every morning.

The food that foxes, raccoons, birds, and other animals consume all winter gives them fuel to keep their bodies warm. The food you and I eat also warms us and gives us energy so that we can have fun in the cold weather. We also keep warm by dressing in layers of clothing and by going into our cozy houses whenever it gets too cold outside.

Some animals, like snakes and wood-chucks, don't eat or try to stay warm in winter. Instead they sleep all winter long. Their bodies actually cool off, and their hearts beat much more slowly, to conserve energy. These animals are hibernating in the frosty soil under my cabin. Can you find them all?

In winter the snow covers the land like a white blanket. The hibernating animals are down under the deepening snow. Animals that remain active all winter can use the snow to nestle into and shelter them from winter wind.

I take out my trusty snowshoes to keep me from sinking down in the fluffy snow as I go for my daily walks.

One winter day I snowshoed into the forest and came upon a flock of wild turkeys. They looked so much like the forest itself, I nearly missed seeing them. How many turkeys do you see here?

With each new snowfall, the white, wintery blanket of snow becomes a layer thicker. My snowshoe trail gets covered and filled in by new snowflakes. And I have to go out and make a new trail!

The wild creatures do the same thing. Each new snowfall is quickly marked by hundreds of fresh new animal tracks.

Animal tracks in the snow always tell a story. Follow these tracks around my cabin and see what stories you can read!

OWL PRINTS · OWL SWOOPING DOWN ~ · WING PRINTS ~

DEER ~ · BEAR ~

The beaver pond looks different in winter. Now it's frozen and covered with snow. Only the surface of a pond freezes. That's why it can be dangerous to walk on frozen ponds. If the surface ice is too thin, you can fall through into the cold water beneath.

ICE

HIBERNATORS
IN
MUD UNDER POND

When I visit the beaver pond in winter, I stay well up on the shore. Sometimes I see animals, like snowshoe rabbits, running over the frozen pond. Small animals are so lightweight, they cannot fall through the ice.

I like to look at the beaver lodge all covered with snow and try to imagine the beavers inside.

Beavers are safe and warm in their lodge. They leave only to swim under the ice to their food supply, which they stored on the bottom of the pond during the busy fall.

A Crinkleroot Nature Quiz

Have you ever wondered what the inside of animal homes look like?

Here are four wildlife homes in winter.

a

See if you can guess whose homes they are.

b

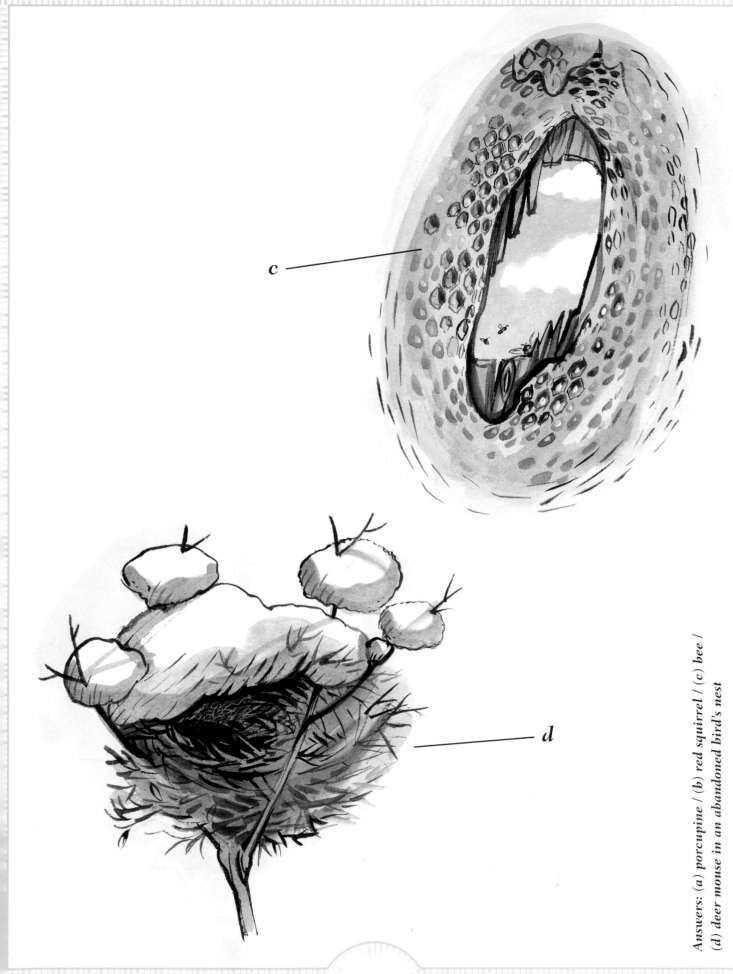

c

d

Answers: (a) porcupine / (b) red squirrel / (c) bee / (d) deer mouse in an abandoned bird's nest

This snow-covered field can be a busy place. Look at all the tracks—cat tracks, fox tracks, and dog tracks. It looks like all three were out romping together. But most likely each set of tracks was made at a different time.

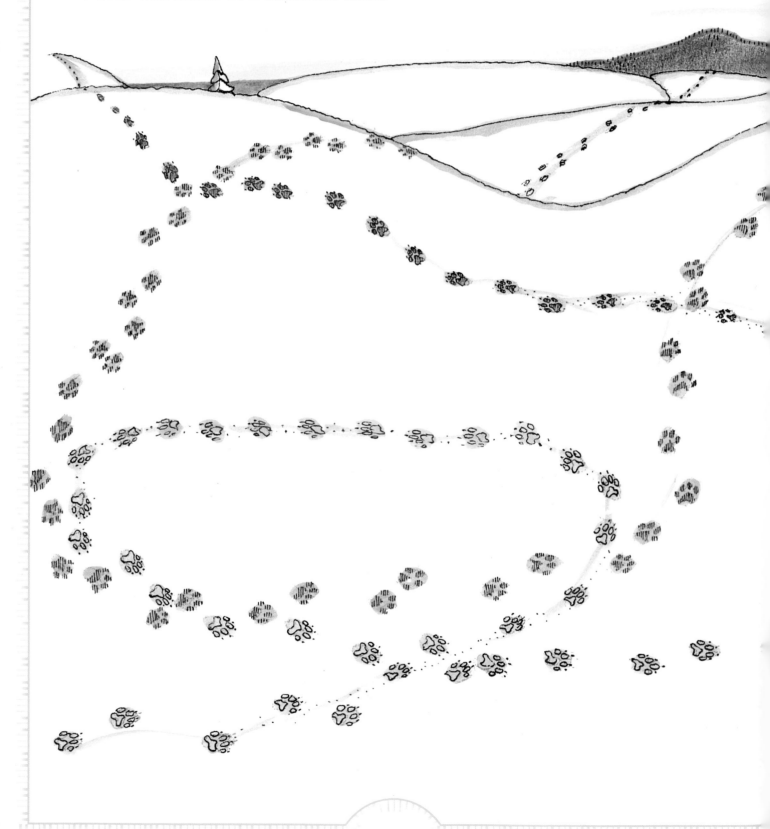

When you see the snow covered with hundreds of tracks, remember each set was probably made by a lone animal walking or running at a time when none of the other track makers were around. Hmm. These tracks look very different from the other tracks in the snow. These are the tracks of a snowshoe rabbit!

SNOWSHOE RABBIT

Where I live the most common rabbit is the snowshoe rabbit.

Snowshoe rabbits are sometimes called "varying hares" because their color varies, or changes, with the seasons. In summer they are brown and blend with the browns and greens of the forest. In winter their fur turns as white as snow, and you can hardly see them. They can hide from enemies by standing still in the snow.

🐾 SNOW SHOE RABBITS ARE MEMBERS OF THE HARE FAMILY.

🐾 SNOWSHOE RABBITS WEIGH ABOUT 5 POUNDS.

🐾 THEY LIVE IN TANGLY PATCHES OF BUSHES AND WOODS.

🐾 THEY EAT GRASSES AND WEEDS IN THE SUMMER AND BARK IN THE WINTER.

Can you find six snowshoe rabbits in this picture?

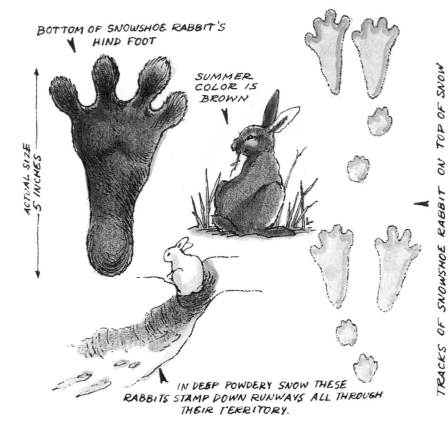

BOTTOM OF SNOWSHOE RABBIT'S HIND FOOT

ACTUAL SIZE 5 INCHES

SUMMER COLOR IS BROWN

TRACKS OF SNOWSHOE RABBIT ON TOP OF SNOW

IN DEEP POWDERY SNOW THESE RABBITS STAMP DOWN RUNWAYS ALL THROUGH THEIR TERRITORY.

These critters are called snowshoe rabbits because of their great big hind feet. See how big and wide they are— just like my own snowshoes! Their large feet keep them up on the snow. It's easier to escape predators if you can run on top of the snow instead of slogging through it.

I've seen a lot of tracks here in the forest—raccoon, deer, fox, snowshoe rabbit, to name a few. But I can't seem to recognize these tracks right next to my own. Why, they must be yours!

Here are the tracks of some common wildlife. All you need to enjoy animal tracks is one footprint.

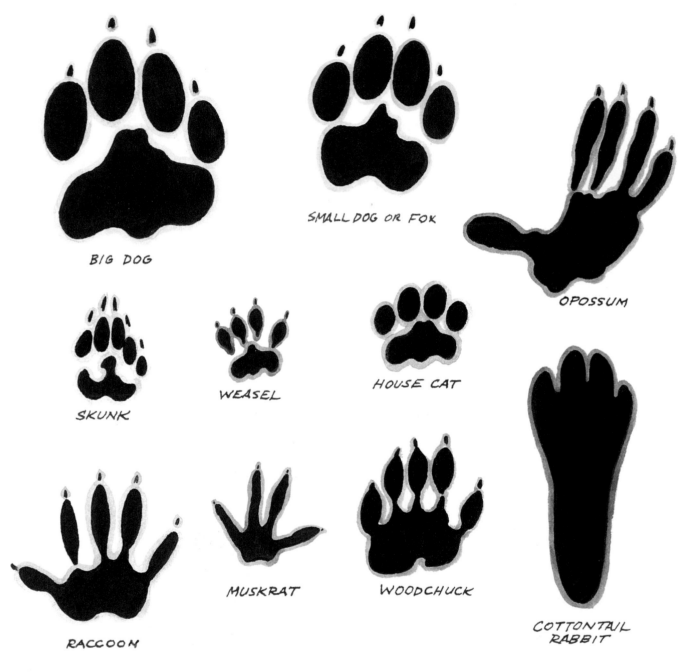

BIG DOG

SMALL DOG OR FOX

OPOSSUM

SKUNK

WEASEL

HOUSE CAT

RACCOON

MUSKRAT

WOODCHUCK

COTTONTAIL RABBIT

MOUSE

CHIPMUNK

Each print shows exactly how the animal's foot is shaped, how many toes it has, and how long and sharp its toenails or claws are.

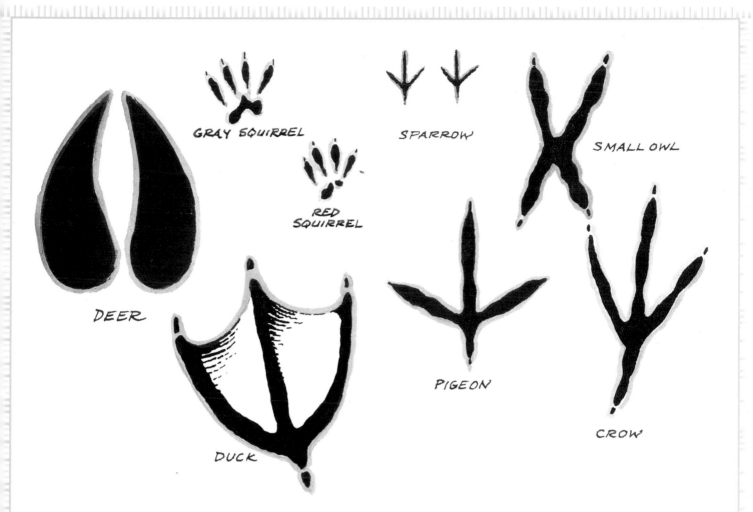

GRAY SQUIRREL

SPARROW

SMALL OWL

RED SQUIRREL

DEER

DUCK

PIGEON

CROW

The next time you are at the seashore or beach, check out your own barefoot prints. They'll show you how your own foot is shaped and how you place each foot as you walk.

THIS IS WHAT CRINKLEROOT'S BARE FOOT PRINT LOOKS LIKE. (LIKE YOURS!)

CRINKLEROOT WALKING BAREFOOT
(THE LITTLE ROUND MARKS ARE MADE BY HIS STICK)

Wherever you live, there are animals living near you. Look for the signs animals leave in parks and playgrounds, on pavement and sidewalks, under trees, around streams and ponds, and in the snow.

If you want to bring wildlife to your own backyard, leave a spot unmowed in your lawn so it can grow wild. Small animals will make their homes in it. Let it be a refuge for the rabbits, deer, and birds who need a place to hide during the day and a place to sleep at night.

I'm glad *I* don't have to sleep outdoors tonight! My toasty woodstove will keep me warm. And it won't be long before I'll be smelling spring in the wind as the circle of seasons turns.

Remember there are pictures everywhere, puzzles hidden among the leaves and in the streams, and stories written on the snow.

So keep your eyes open and your nose poked out, and someday you may be talking caterpillar, turtle, and salamander!

CRINKLEROOT

HATBAND

WALKING STICK

MOCCASINS

🐾 CRINKLEROOT WAS BORN IN A TREE AND RAISED BY BEES.

🐾 HE CAN WHISTLE IN A HUNDRED LANGUAGES AND SPEAK CATERPILLAR, SALAMANDER, AND TURTLE.

🐾 HE KNOWS ALL ABOUT WILD ANIMALS, EVEN THE ONES THAT LIVE AROUND YOUR HOUSE!